THE SLOTH WHO COULD NOT SLEEP

First published by EUOI Press, London 2011
Also available in digital editions for Kindle and iBooks
www.euoipress.com

Cover design by Yeomans, www.yeomanscreative.co.uk
Printed and bound by Lightning Source on SFI certified paper
Typeset in Minion Pro 13 / 16
ISBN 978-1-908100-03-0

The Sloth Who Could Not Sleep

A Fable

by

Samantha Brenton

EUOI Press

In memory of Ralph Caplan

Contents

CHAPTER ONE
The Rude Awakening

Dylan dangled from the top branch of his bold skyscraper tree. His four paws, with their very long claws, gripped the bark securely. Plump raindrops spiralled down his dark green, mouldy, wiry hair and then cascaded to the ground below. Even though it was raining (yet again) his bulbous eyes enjoyed scanning the top of the rainforest, with its vast flourishing trees waving back at him, mounted by a silk pale blue sky and lit by a saffron-coloured sun. On this day there was a mesmerising rainbow curtsying to him overhead. He never tired of the view when he was awake. But as a three-toed sloth he was a tired a lot of the time, and needed an astonishing eighteen hours of sleep, or so, each day.

He was in a dilemma about whether or not to travel down his tree. He did this once a week, begrudgingly and extremely slowly, to go to the toilet. The other option was to have a little bit more napping time. The napping-for-a-little-while-longer option won, as the toilet time was not an urgent issue. Each time, before sleeping, he ritually touched the names of his mother and father that were etched on the tree trunk behind his head. The etching had been done by his parents before they left him whilst he was asleep a few years ago, leaving him to live an independent life. He felt close to them and less alone when he ran a paw over their names on the bark before shutting his eyes.

With a belly full of cecropia leaves and curled up in a comfortable position he closed his eyes and began to drift off. He always relished that drowsy state before his surroundings and thoughts were drawn into the sleepy abyss. Just as he was almost there, he was disturbed by a loud noise.

'CHOP! CHOP! CHOP! CHOP! CHOP!'

His branch swayed from side to side with every chopping sound. The exotic birds, with their fat yellow chests and bills, took flight. Dylan held on tightly to his branch and looked up to see the flashes of colour from the birds above, then turned his head downwards and squinted to see what was causing the disturbance. At the bottom of the tree were two creatures that he had never seen before: one tall and slender and the other small and portly. They both held sharp objects attached to long sticks and stood with a confident stance, knees bent, squatting with their bottoms sticking out. They hacked with determination at the base of the tree. Sweat poured off their brows and their nostrils flared.

Dylan felt terrified. What could he do? Where

could he go?

They put down their tools. The motion of the tree stopped and he let out a sigh of relief. However, the silence was short lived. One of them picked up a hefty instrument made of a shiny material and got back to work. Dylan's branch shook uncontrollably, an aggressive sound roared and the mechanical appendage sliced through the trunk with ease.

'Vvvvvvvvvvvvvvrrrrrrrrrrrrrrrrrrrrrrrrrrrrrrmmmmmmmmmmmmmmm!'

Once again the forest fell silent for a few seconds. A voice shouted, 'TIMBER!'

Dylan had no chance to escape. He clung tightly to the branch as the tree came crashing diagonally to the ground. It collapsed in a matter of seconds but, for Dylan, the descent seemed to be in slow motion. His whole life flashed before his eyes.

He was thrown violently and ricocheted off a tree trunk. Luckily, a pile of leaves and mosses cushioned his landing. He lay there on his back in shock for some time, then cautiously looked around to establish if the same had happened to the trees surrounding him. To his astonishment the other trees stood tall and proud exactly where they were before, unharmed. All but his tree: his home.

The tall and small figures strutted away merrily leaving an eerie silence behind them. Dylan started to cry. He was homeless and, for the first time in his life, felt very uncertain. With a throbbing pain in his head, he sat up and brushed himself down to rid of the moist leaves that smothered him from head to paw.

He looked around anxiously not knowing what to do or where to go. Then, through the silence came a familiar voice that spoke to him.

'Dylan? Dylan? Are you in one piece?' It was the distinguished voice of Dylan's neighbour, Oscar. 'Are you alright, Chico?'

Dylan turned his head and came eye to eye with Oscar hanging upside down by his hind legs from a tree branch next to him. Oscar was a sloth like himself, but he took much more pride in his appearance, with combed grey hair and an autumnal coloured cravat of leaves around his neck.

Dylan took a moment to squish his faculties back together, sighed and said shakily, 'Yes, I think so. I… I… I… haven't a clue what just happened to me. Oh, it's so good to see your friendly face, Oscar.'

'It looked rather dramatic from where I was hanging,' Oscar explained. 'One minute I'm having a peaceful sleep and the next a loud noise awoke me. My hearing is useless, apparently, so it must have been incredibly loud to bring me out of my doze. 1… 2… 3… THUD! Your tree crashed to the ground. I blinked and it was gone. I've never felt so frightened. It was those humans, you know. I'd only ever heard of scary tales like that but never thought it would happen here where we live! Your tree is no longer in its space. How can that be?'

Dylan mumbled, 'I really don't know. Nothing

makes sense at the moment, Oscar. Would it be okay to share your tree branch for now? I have nowhere else to go.'

'Sure, Chico,' replied Oscar. 'It would be my pleasure but I must warn you that I have been accused of snoring before.'

Dylan went to the loo discreetly - as he was now on the forest floor - and climbed very slowly up the tree trunk to the first branch and hung upside down next to Oscar. He closed his eyes and tried to sleep, but to no avail. He wriggled around and tried to get comfortable but was still unsuccessful. His failed attempt to sleep had nothing to do with Oscar's snoring, even though it really was shockingly loud. No, Dylan couldn't sleep because he had a lot of things to think about. The events of that day laid heavily on his mind and everything that he once knew became a puzzle that didn't make sense anymore.

A few hours passed and gradually his exhausted body dictated that he must sleep. His eyelids drooped heavily and closed.

Just as he was about to drift off he felt a twinkling sensation on his nose. He opened one eye but could only see a blur so with a little effort he opened both of his bulbous eyes together. He was very annoyed at being disturbed yet again, but this soon turned to amazement as he focussed on the most beautiful thing he had ever seen.

There it was, small enough to be balancing delicately on his nose and yet a vibrant vision of bright red. With delicate lacy wings flapping and big deep-set green eyes, framed with fluttering long eyelashes, it looked directly at him.

'Hhhelloo,' a tiny voice said.

He couldn't hear too well and so said, 'Sorry, a bit hard of hearing. Can you speak up?'

The creature flew in a zigzag to Dylan's ear and nervously shouted, 'I, I said Hi! Are you the gentleman that used to live in that tree?'

'I hear you now,' replied Dylan. 'Yes, I did live in that tree - all my life. Why?'

'I've been sent here to investigate what has just happened.'

'Who are you?' enquired Dylan.

'Oh how rude of me. I'm Viva, a butterfly,' her elegant voice replied. 'I know exactly what you are. You are one of those sleepy sloth creatures but do you have a name, sleepy sloth?'

'My name is Dylan.'

'Right, Dylan, my job is to get to the bottom of this situation so please tell me all you can remember. There's no rush, so think carefully about every detail.'

With that, Viva produced a pencil and notepad from under her wing and began to scribble down Dylan's words.

'Well,' he began, 'I woke up at about midday and ate cecropia leaves for about two hours on my branch. I then felt tired again and so decided to have a nap. At about mid-afternoon I was disturbed by an enormous jolt and a strange noise, and in a matter of minutes I was clinging on for dear life. Then the tree fell with me securely attached to it. I'm okay though. Perhaps a bit shaken up,' he said trying to mask his fear with a brave face.

'Did you see what was responsible for the destruction?' Viva questioned.

'A-ha,' Dylan nodded. 'It was those humans, I think they are called? The ones that I'd only ever heard about in stories but never thought I'd see up close. They hacked away at the base of the tree then shouted 'TIMBER!'. The tree fell and they walked away rather happy with themselves. I don't know what I've done to make them do such a thing.'

'Oh, these incidents are becoming more and more common throughout the forest. I'm sure that it wasn't anything that you did wrong,' she comforted.

'I have just a few more questions, Dylan, if you don't mind? Now, you've said that you ate and slept before this occurred. Did you do anything else? For instance, leave your branch? Talk to anyone? Eat something other than cecropia leaves? Groom yourself?'

After some challenging thought, Dylan replied, 'Um… um… no. I don't tend to do any of those things regularly in my daily routine.'

'How interesting, and slightly peculiar, I must add.' Viva sounded a bit bemused. 'Well, thank you Dylan for your co-operation. I must be going now to further my investigation. You don't happen to know the way to Lake Aromatza?' she asked with a friendly lopsided smile.

'Err, no sorry, I don't know what Lake Aromatza is,' Dylan answered.

'Silly me, I naturally assumed you'd be a global traveller like myself,' she boasted.

'No, I don't really travel further than up and down my tree or occasionally I may venture to another branch. I wasn't built with wings like you. So what now? About my tree, that is.'

'Dylan, there are too many cases like yours occurring in the forest nowadays and I'm going to get to the bottom of it. My instincts are telling me that I must head to Lake Aromatza. When I know more, I shall return and inform you of my findings. Until then, I suggest you continue with your usual routine of... um... hanging around.'

They looked at each other for a few seconds and Dylan tried to think of something else to say but before he could say anything else, Viva put away her notepad and pencil and produced a mirror from behind her wing. She looked intently into it, stroking her eyelashes and precisely positioning each one.

'How do I look?' she asked, pouting glamorously.

Dylan replied, 'Err, very nice, Viva.'

She snapped the mirror shut and placed it back under her wing. 'I, I'd better be fluttering by. Thank you for allowing me to land on your snout and for being so helpful.' And with that she flew away towards a burnt orange sun that was now setting over the forest.

'B, Bye,' Dylan shouted after her but he realised she probably didn't hear him. 'Wait!' he shouted, but it was too late: she had vanished.

As the sun had started sinking towards the horizon, it was now time to eat, but he didn't feel hungry. He didn't feel tired either and just hung from the tree with heavy rain dripping off of him, thinking about what had just happened.

'Sleep, sleep, sleep... You know that you're the best at it, so sleeeeep!' he muttered to himself. But no matter how hard he tried, twisting and turning, he realised that his mind was wondering about what had just happened. He felt a deep need to see the butterfly again, and know where she was going and why. So he made a life-changing resolution, unheard of in the sloth world: he decided to go on an adventure to find Viva.

Dylan needed to wake Oscar to tell him of his plans and reached over to tickle his friend on his stomach. It took plenty of persistence but finally Oscar woke.

'Ha? Hey? Hmmm? Who's that?' Oscar mumbled, confused. He opened his eyes to see Dylan dangling beside him. 'Buenos dias, Dylan! Did you sleep well? Same old, same old routine, hey Chico?'

Dylan drew a deep breath in and began, 'Good to see you, Oscar. Thank you for your hospitality but I feel very restless at the moment and I've decided to, well, I'm going on an adventure actually. Heading that way,' he said pointing in the direction in which the butterfly had flown.

Concerned, Oscar said, 'Are you sure you should be leaving the comfort of this part of the forest? I mean no one knows what's out there, beyond these trees around us. It's, it's SCARY!'

'That is exactly why I'm going, Oscar. When I plummeted from the height of my branch, my whole life flashed before my eyes and, to be truly honest, there really wasn't too much to see. I saw myself sleeping, eating and having an occasional chat but that was pretty much it. While you were sleeping, I met a butterfly who is doing some undercover work and it sounded contagiously exciting. I want to see how other beings live in this vast and flourishing forest and perhaps it will answer some questions about why I lost my home,' responded Dylan, who was now feeling a bit anxious but knew he mustn't turn back or he'd always regret it.

'Rather you than me,' Oscar chortled. 'Skulking suits me just fine. Just the thought of a faster pace makes me feel nauseous. Give me my space and home comforts any day. I get a thrill just comparing the different purples of the evening sky from here. I'll await your return. Take best care of yourself, dear Chico.'

With that, Oscar retired once again and Dylan was left alone, filled with anticipation. For the first time he realised the scale of what he was about to do.

'No time for nerves, Dylan, me boy,' he thought

to himself and looked down at the hive of activity amongst the leaves and shrubs.

He realised that finding a quicker mode of transport was a matter of urgency, as he knew that he, being a sloth, could only travel extremely slowly. 'There is always a lot of movement below me on the forest floor so I'll head down there,' he thought.

Slowly he moved down the trunk and some time later reached ground level, breathless.

CHAPTER TWO
Rar, Rar, Rainforest

An army of ants marched past carrying large leaf-cuttings, berries and nuts on their backs.

'Quick march, Privates! There's no time for slacking. Left, right, left, right, LEFT!' ordered the General leading the troops.

Dylan overheard one of the ants complaining, 'Oh, this berry is much too heavy for an ant of my ripe old age. My back is killing me!'

Dylan decided to help out the tiny insect and removed the berry from its back with the sharp tip of one of his claws. The ant continued on the march and, when it sensed that the burden had been lifted from its posterior, it looked back and gave Dylan a very grateful wink.

Dylan had never eaten a berry and decided to try it for the first time. At first, he gave it a little lick, then put it in his mouth to suck and finally chewed and swallowed.

'Hmmm, intriguing taste sensation. A bit sweet

for my palate,' he thought, as a gratified smile spread across his face.

The moment could not be savoured for long as an unfamiliar, odd, utterly stern creature with an angular, seaweed-green face looked him directly in the eye.

The strange animal coughed to clear his throat and said, 'Good Evening, Sir. I'm Trevor, a tortoise, and this is my family. We are on holiday and have travelled a great distance, floating on a log across the sea and hiking for miles across the land. Would it be okay with you if we camped here by this tree for the night?'

'Sure,' replied Dylan, 'I live here but I'm actually heading that way myself to explore.'

'We're heading in the same direction, so why don't you let us have a little shut eye and when the sun rises you can join us for some travel companionship?'

Dylan thought that was a perfect idea, 'Terrific! But would it be of any inconvenience for me to hitch a ride on your shell? My movement is rather sluggish, you see.'

'No problem,' replied Trevor, 'Nighty night for now!'

And with that, his head and feet disappeared into his enormous dome, with its tapestry of various earthy green and brown colouring. The female tortoise gathered the children together and all three smiled at Dylan and then disappeared under their armour.

Dylan reflected that, although a lot had happened since the sunset, he actually hadn't travelled any further than to the bottom of a tree. He was excited for the day ahead. Feeling more awake than ever he prepared a feast of his favourite cecropia leaves from the ground and contently munched, appreciating the sumptuous juicy flavours. He raised his eyes to the sky and waited anxiously for the stars and moon to be replaced with bright daylight. It seemed a long wait and he was feeling tired but unable to snooze.

The first of the family to wake was Trevor. He gently tapped on the shells of his female companion and children.

'Wakey, wakey, rise and shine!'

Trevor then became impatient and the gentle tapping turned to vigorous knocking, as if playing the bongo drums, but unfortunately lacking in natural rhythm.

'Okay, honey, I'm awake!' said the flustered mother who stirred slowly and peeped out from her shell. The parents were soon joined by their son, but there was no sign of their daughter seeing daylight as she was sleeping deeply. The son decided to roll the sleepy shell around, humming a tune because he knew it would annoy his sister and after some perseverance it worked.

Her head popped out of her shell and she shouted in a prickly tone, 'Get off of me, you brat!' Then she groaned, 'Oh, is it that time already?'

The tortoises spent a while munching slowly on

vegetation for breakfast.

Dylan became frustrated.

Finally when it was all becoming too much, Trevor, his mouth full of breakfast, announced those magic words: 'Right, let's get moving!'

Dylan couldn't contain his excitement and leapt gleefully on the back of Trevor's shell. They set off in the same direction as the butterfly. Dylan closed his eyes tightly but couldn't sleep, too excited in the knowledge that his journey had begun. He sat comfortably cross-legged, closed his eyes and felt his blood whooshing around his body. He listened intently to the sounds of the birds surrounding them, until he could feel the cold on his fur and the pads of his paws which indicated that evening had arrived in the forest. He opened his eyes, smiled and yawned. Mid-yawn, he realised with ghastly astonishment that they had only travelled a very short distance all day. As he looked behind him he could still see Oscar's tree!

'Trevor?' he asked assertively, 'Why are we moving so slowly? I thought you might at least travel a bit faster than I can.'

'Oh, we only travel at this pace. Carrying this heavy shell doesn't allow us to race along. And this way we can take in the scenery,' Trevor replied. 'Why? Does it not suit you, my friend?'

'No, sorry, I forgot to mention that speed is of the essence if I am to meet up with Viva, my butterfly friend.'

A disgruntled Trevor grumpily shook Dylan

off his shell, sending the sloth sliding down the side of the dome, bouncing off a nearby tree and landing awkwardly on his bottom.

'Oooooow! Ouch!'

'I think you'd better find alternative travel arrangements,' said Trevor.

'I didn't mean to offend,' Dylan tried to appease. 'Please, let's remain friends and part on good terms?'

'Okay, okay. Better wish you luck then.'

Trevor sighed and addressed the rest of the family, 'Onwards we go, gang! Bid farewell to Dylan now.'

Four wrinkly faces turned and smiled at Dylan and then wandered away at a not very dramatic pace.

CHAPTER THREE
Moving, Grooving and Munching

Dylan watched the family of tortoises amble away and looked around desperately for a quicker mode of transport.

And there it was: a bigger creature than himself! Its strong, bulging body seemed entirely out of proportion with its four skinny long legs, and its long floppy snout was snuffling for insects amongst the leaves on the ground.

'Hello over there, can you hear me?' Dylan enquired.

The creature stopped and looked over. 'Yep, this must be important for you to disturb my noshing time.'

'Err, sorry about that. My name is Dylan and I'm a sloth on a mission. I could really do with your assistance.'

'I'm Sandra, a tapir, and how can I help you, Dylan, the sloth?'

'I,' Dylan swallowed some saliva and continued,

'I'm a bit speed-challenged and need to head that way,' he said pointing to indicate the direction. 'Would you mind giving me a lift?'

She inspected the stranger from head to claw, paused and replied, 'Yeah, why not? I can go and visit my relatives by the river.'

'Oh, thank you, thank you, thank you,' said Dylan, oozing appreciation.

'No time to waste. Hop on and get cosy because it's a bit of a trek.'

Dylan gathered a big pile of various leaves to eat during the journey, hugged them close to his body and climbed carefully aboard the tapir being careful not to scratch her with his long claws. He placed the pile of leaves behind his head as a pillow and rested on his back with paws in the air. He was feeling ravenous and so he reached behind his head, picked one leaf at a time, and savoured every chew of his mobile picnic.

It was getting dark. With his nocturnal vision the forest seemed a peaceful place, with most of the inhabitants fast asleep. That was until…

'BBBBUNDLE!'

A cheeky shriek was heard nearby and suddenly a ball of gold and black hair came hurtling towards him and landed on his stomach. Yikes. The large ball then divided into three much smaller golden-headed lion tamarins (mini-monkeys the size of squirrels with long, golden, shiny, hippy hairstyles).

Another shriek followed, 'Wait for us, gang!', and two small silvery marmoset identical twins (slightly smaller than the tamarins, with pointy ears, silvery bodies and pixie faces) leapt from a tree branch and landed directly on Dylan's head.

He had seen tamarins and marmosets in the forest before, but had never had anything to do with them as they had far too much energy for his liking. To him their behaviour was quite bonkers.

The marmosets stood on Dylan's head and leaned over to peer into his eyes, one on the left and the other on the right. They then disappeared from his view and after a few seconds somersaulted from his head and landed in front of him on top of the three tamarins' shoulders to form a primate pyramid.

The tamarin in the centre addressed him, 'Greetings my travelling friend! Let me introduce you to your in-house entertainment for this trip. To my left is Fantastic Tina, to my right is Invincible Vince, above are the marvellous marmoset twins Amber and Ruby, and my name is Goldie. Now, you sit back and relax while we give you the greatest show on Earth and we'll discuss payment afterwards.'

Dylan became flustered and asked, 'Before you begin, I must state that I have nothing to pay you with, nothing at all.'

Goldie replied, 'Absolute nonsense. You have lots of delicious mites and other yummy insects for us to indulge ourselves on, living within your untamed hair.'

'I never knew that,' said Dylan. 'So, in that case, let the show commence!'

Sandra interrupted, 'Is everything okay back there?' She was unaware of the crazy activity that was happening on her hide.

'Yes, just fine, thank you,' responded Dylan, who then winked at Goldie to start the performance.

A chorus of crickets flew down and, by rubbing their back wings together at different speeds, provided the music for the acrobatic show. They were joined by fireflies who flew above, turned on their fluorescent abdomens, and lit Dylan's pot belly as a temporary stage.

Goldie took centre stage while the others of the crew stood aside. He produced a number of brightly coloured berries from behind his back and began to juggle: first three berries, then four berries and then five berries, with a look of determined concentration on his face. His eyebrows moved up and down rapidly.

'Ta-dah!' he announced as he caught them all together in his long bony digits.

Dylan's happiness was uncontrollable and he laughed and clapped along.

The other tamarins joined the act and at supersonic speed juggled the berries between all three of them, all the time changing positions and posture, throwing the berries from under their legs, over their heads, behind their backs and everywhere. The berries travelled at such a pace that they produced streaks of colour similar to a firework display.

Dylan was captivated.

Next, the marmoset twins performed an acrobatic act that they had practised to perfection, with cartwheels, somersaults next to each other, on each other, over each other. Hop… skip… twirl… curtsy…

'Wow!' Dylan thought. 'They are so small and agile.'

All five then lined up and performed a dance routine while twirling twigs with brightly coloured strands of grass attached, spectacularly synchronised; a swing to the left, a turn to the right, the sticks went above their heads, behind their backs and down to the floor.

The finale was the best bit of all. There was a drum roll as one by one they leapt on one another's shoulders to form one tall primate pillar, slightly wobbly and swaying with Sandra's strides. Tina curtsied at the top. They all smiled, a column of very white teeth shining through the darkness.

Dylan clapped and giggled, 'Wow, you guys and girls, that was incredible. You make it look so easy.'

'Years of practice,' said the shyest of the three, blushing.

'Do you think I could do it?' enquired Dylan.

'No offence, mate,' replied Goldie, 'but I don't think you're built in the same way as us, so NO! You'd look totally ridiculous, in my opinion. Anyway, there are too many primates in this business already. Stick to what you're good at, that's my motto. Come on crew, tuck in!'

Dylan felt a bit sad as he reflected on Goldie's comment, knowing that there wasn't anything he considered himself being particularly good or gifted at, but this glum thought was quickly dispelled by five ravenous primates who had earned their right to feast on the bugs that made themselves at home in his hair. They carefully parted areas of his body and with wide eyes eagerly removed various moving things and ate them.

'You see,' said Vince, with a mouthful of moving insects, 'your talent is to provide the most delicious cuisine that I have ever tasted in this forest.' A grub managed to escape from his mouth as he talked, and made a quick escape down his chin to freedom.

Dylan was delighted to hear such a comment and realised that he didn't even have to make any effort to provide the buffet that pleased his new companions. Their nibbling also produced a soothing massaging sensation as they sieved through his matted hair.

The journey continued without conversation as they feasted and Dylan munched on his leaves. The only sounds to be heard were the pitter-patter of falling rain on the forest leaves and the occasional call of a bird of paradise.

The saffron sunrise crept up. The tamarins and marmosets huddled together on his stomach and fell asleep.

Dylan really wanted to snooze but time ticked by and he could only rest with droopy eyes. His mind just wouldn't switch off; he yearned to swirl into that familiar abyss but something was preventing him.

'Dylan, oh Dylan,' Sandra whispered. 'Open your eyes and look at this.'

He opened his eyes, gave them a rub and turned to look. He saw a beautiful sight.

The pitter-patter of rain was landing gently on the river, forming large fresh droplet circles on the surface of the murky water. There were pretty plants, pink and purple, growing around and within the river. Some were large lily pads, so large that Dylan could easily have sprawled on one and used it as a bed. He daydreamed about relishing his favourite pastime - sleeping - on one of them, as he hadn't had any luck anywhere else yet, but it was just wishful thinking. It was a breathtaking scene. The lotus flowers were meditating on the water.

Sandra stopped to snuffle on some vegetation and vacuum up some insects whilst Dylan enjoyed doing nothing at all. He just watched metallic drag-onflies busying themselves just above the water and allowed his senses to soak it all up. The rest of the mobile entourage were still asleep and Dylan wanted to enjoy the peace. No talking, no movement, just peaceful stillness as he appreciated the surroundings that he had never really experienced before in his home tree. Enchanted.

After some time, Sandra looked up and called for Dylan. He leaned over so they were face to face.

'This is the end of the road for me, young man. My relatives live down there to the right.'

She then realised that Dylan was not her only passenger.

'Hey, what are they doing on my back?!'

She glared at the gold and silver fur balls, perturbed.

Dylan replied, 'They just made themselves comfy and to be honest, Sandra, they have made my trip quite eventful. Perhaps I should have told you. I am truly, truly sorry.' He frowned nervously.

She replied, starting quietly and getting louder and louder, 'Right, well, it's time for you all to be on your way. Go on! Be off with you! Hop it! Shoo! Shoo!'

Dylan ruffled the primates on his belly and told them it was time to disembark.

'Right you are, Sir Sloth,' said Goldie.

They lined up in a row and one after the other somersaulted off Dylan's midriff. He rolled onto his stomach and slid down the tapir to the forest floor.

Dylan faced Sandra and acknowledged, 'Thank you dearly for being so kind as to carry me here. You really are a gracious lady.'

Sandra blushed and coyly responded, 'Oh, go away. It really was nothing. Hope to catch up with you some time as I know where you live now, Dylan the sloth.'

Dylan replied, 'That would be lovely. You'd be welcome anytime.'

'You have to head across the river if you want to continue in that direction,' she advised.

He watched as she strutted elegantly away, then realised what she had just said: he would have to cross the river.

Gulp.

'Aaaaarrrrghhh! Panic!'

He felt frozen in his tracks, and thought to himself, 'It's alright for butterflies. They can just fly across with great ease but what about a chunky sloth without useful things like wings?'

The acrobats meanwhile were dangling from his hair and misbehaving, playfully biting, pinching and punching each other.

'Hey, party crew!' He addressed them enthusiastically, 'How do you fancy crossing the river with me?'

Their activity halted and they looked at each other, wide-eyed.

Goldie assertively said, 'Have you gone mad? No thanks. We primates despise getting soaked to the skin. Come on gang, it's time to be off!' And with that they all made a speedy dash for the nearest tree, cackling with laughter.

Dylan moved towards the river's edge. He peered into the water and saw his reflection for the very first time.

'Cor, you look a mess,' he observed, 'but generally not a bad looking sloth.'

He attempted to comb his untamed hair using

his long claws. It seemed to spray out in every direction: not a handsome sight.

While he was grooming himself he looked to his right and witnessed the most unusual display. There seemed to be a congregation of six boa constrictor snakes participating in an exercise class, led by the most slender of the group, hissing her instructions with a thick lisp. The teacher's long tongue wobbled in the air with every word.

Dylan watched, fascinated.

'Now classssss, twisst to the right. Yesss, as far as you can go. Hold it 5-4-3-2-1 and releasssse. Now, the other sssside, twisssst your coilsss to the left. Hold it 5-4.'

Dylan overheard one of the snakes moan to its neighbour, 'Oh, I wish I hadn't eaten such a big lunch. I'm stuffed! I can't breathe, let alone move!'

Dylan could see the shape of what looked like a bird in its middle.

The instructor interrupted, 'No talking pleasssse at the back there. Now, everyone sssstretch up to the ssssssky - assss tall assss you can go. Headssss up and hold. Remember: no pain, no gain!'

A butterfly flew past Dylan and for a split second he thought it might have been Viva, but it wasn't. This butterfly had brown, yellow and green colouring and certainly wasn't as delightful as the one he was searching for. He felt awkward and out of place.

'Now, how am I to cross this river?' Dylan thought to himself. 'Maybe this is as far as I can go?

Give up now. I mean, you've had a bit of an adventure anyway.'

In that short moment of doubt, he overheard an interesting conversation.

'Excuse me! Hello! Cooeee!'

Dylan looked over to his left and saw a shimmering pale green and fairly large iguana who was talking to the water.

'Yes, Ma'am, can I 'elp ya?' replied a voice from the river.

Dylan squinted to block out the sun's glare and focus on where the reply was coming from.

'Caiman Cabs at ya service, Ma'am,' said a rugged, prehistoric and certainly sinister creature with a long mouthful of unruly teeth.

The iguana continued, 'Well, there's a rather nice looking chap over the other side of the river and he's waving his large and bold red chin flap which indicates that he'd like to meet me. I know I am able to swim but I would much rather he saw me arriving in style, so any chance of a lift over there?'

The caiman glanced over and said, 'It would be me pleasure, Ma'am. Hop on me back and ya'll be there in nay time.'

The glamorous iguana used the caiman's snout as a boarding ramp, walked over his head, turned around and reversed astride his spine so they faced the same way. Encouraged, Dylan watched as the caiman glided across the water towards the far riverbank, its muscular tail swishing behind him, with the iguana on its back.

When they reached the other side, she stepped off confidently, using his snout more like a catwalk this time. She posed for a moment with her long tail swishing behind her and sashayed towards the male iguana. They couldn't take their eyes off each other and his red chin flapped more vigourously with every step that she took towards him.

Dylan thought to himself, 'There's no need to let a river stop me. I can't believe I was going to be such a coward.'

The caiman returned to Dylan's side of the river and lifted his glassy dark brown eyes just above the water's surface to peer at the sloth. He seemed somewhat creepy and Dylan was unsure whether to approach him. I mean, it's one thing to give another reptile a lift, but a sloth might have made for interesting food, considering the dietary needs of a caiman.

Before Dylan had a chance to scurry away from the edge, the caiman snorted in a low pitched, earthshaking grumble, 'Can I 'elp ya, Guvna?'

CHAPTER FOUR
Slothstroke

Dylan opened his mouth but nothing came out. He was speechless with fear.

'Ah, ya're worried I might wanna eat ya, aren't ya?' said the caiman.

'Don't worry 'bout that, young fella. The wife 'as got me on a low fat eating regime so I only eat little and often. Sloths are too fattening for me nowadays, and I wanna to 'ave a long and 'elfy life. We can live well over 100 years if we look after ourselves, ya know', the voice reasoned.

Dylan nodded in agreement but still felt distrustful.

'I'm heading towards Lake Aromatza and I think I need to cross the river to get there. Any chance of a lift?'

The caiman answered slowly, 'Well yeah, Lake Aromatza is that way, so ya do 'ave to cross 'ere, young fella. Why does a sloth like ya wanna 'ead there anyways?'

Dylan explained about trying to find Viva and the adventure he had embarked upon. 'You see, I'm learning new things about myself and this forest all the time,' he concluded.

'In that case,' chattered the caiman, 'I 'ave anuvver travel surprise for ya, young fella. Ya don't need the services of Caiman Cabs, at all. Didn't ya know that sloths can swim? In fact, ya can swim pretty well indeed. Better than ya can walk.'

Dylan couldn't believe his ears.

'No, you're winding me up,' he said.

'Nah, 'onestly, ya really can swim. We don't see many of ya sloths 'round 'ere but I can recall a few years back now, there was a sloth that came to the river and swam as well as a fish – a hairy fish that is. So stop pondering about it, get in this warm water and I'll give ya yer first swimming lesson.'

Dylan rolled his eyes and said, 'Oh, okay, but you have to promise that you won't take your eyes off me for one second, in case I get into any trouble.'

'It's a deal,' replied the caiman reassuringly.

Dylan started off very slowly at the edge of the riverbank, one paw and then the other.

'The water feels quite cold to me,' he said nervously.

'Oh, it's lovely once ya're in. Come on, young fella,' coached the caiman.

Dylan noticed something rusty moving in the river, 'What's that moving under the water?'

'That's a shoal of piranhas,' the caiman answered.

Dylan panicked, 'I've heard nasty things about them. No way. No way am I getting in with flesh-eating fish around me.'

He reversed back from the edge.

'Don't be so silly,' the caiman spoke wisely. 'These piranhas won't hurt ya. Firstly, despite what most creatures fink, the piranha is a sensitive and fussy fish. Secondly, they've 'ad a good feed recently and so won't be 'ungry for days and, firdly, they won't bovver snacking on ya as ya've got too much matted 'air to chew frough. Now get in!'

Dylan took a slow deep breath and a few foot-steps later he was submerged up to his neck in murky water.

'Now, paddle like ya're walking on land but fast-er,' instructed the caiman.

Dylan moved with all four limbs flailing in dif-ferent directions.

'Not so erratically! Get a rhyfm going and relax. Ya'll start to enjoy it.'

Dylan did as he was told and, astonishingly, started moving in the direction of the other riverbank. The caiman swam next to him, beaming with pride at being the one to teach Dylan such an essential skill.

'Don't forget to breaffe, young fella.'

Dylan started to enjoy the sensation of the water seeping between his hair strands. It was cool and pro-vided an excellent relief to his itchy skin.

'Hmmm, this is lovely!' he exclaimed with a look of concentration on his face.

'Yer 'alf way there so no turning back now,' the caiman continued, 'how do ya fancy gettin' yer 'ead wet as well?'

Dylan took a deep breath and in a moment of bravery sank totally under the water.

He could see all the fish swimming around him and it was an incredible revelation for one who had always been on land. He lifted his head and realised he was almost at the other side. Slowing down, he approached the riverbank and climbed back on land again, digging his claws into the soil.

'Hooray! I did it. Feeling a bit out of breath but brilliant, that's for sure,' he said triumphantly.

'Well done, ya were an easy student, young fella.'

'I couldn't have done it without you coaching me. Cheers!'

'Ya did all the work. But this is just the beginning. Ya must practise and it'll get even better until ya get like me and don't even 'ave to fink about it.'

Their conversation was interrupted.

'Do you mind?' spoke an annoyed voice, bluntly.

They both looked over in the direction of a rather aggravated praying mantis. Its twiggy leaf-like insect body was by no means a threat to the caiman or sloth. However, it had large dark eyes, which took up the majority of its face, and they expressed displeasure at being disturbed.

'I'm trying to take a martial arts class over here by this tranquil river but if you're going to continue yapping we may just have to find another location.'

'So sorry,' said the caiman, 'didn't mean to offend ya.'

He whispered to Dylan, 'Well, I'd better get back to work anyway. Some rainforest creatures aren't as gifted in the water as us. Take it easy, Swimming Sloth.'

The caiman lowered his head so only his eyes were visible. He blinked his left eye and then the right, and swam away, thrashing his strong tail behind him.

CHAPTER FIVE
The Calm Before the Storm

Alone again, he was curious to watch the martial arts class that he had disturbed. It looked intriguing. A line of praying mantises faced forward with focussed, almost possessed, eyes. The instructor moved in silence and was mirrored accurately by all the participants. Dylan could hear them clearly even though they were minute in size; insect noises were high-pitched enough for him to listen in.

'Now remember, class, deep relaxing breaths, clear your mind of any troubles and focus on the movement. Nice, slow and accurate. Breathe in and place the left arm in front of you, the right arm bent and close to your ear, and luuuuuunnnnge.'

All the heads of the class looked disdainfully towards the dripping wet sloth. Even though they were much smaller than him, he felt quite intimidated by their stares. They turned away from him and faced front with hands in the praying position and bowed to the instructor.

'Now, split into pairs.'

They all paired off and began to practise fighting each other one-on-one. One would kick and the other block. Then punch and block. Their leafy limbs cut gracefully through the air. All accompanied with deep vocal fighting sounds: 'Huh!' 'Ha-sowww!'

One pair wasn't as keen to fight and subtly did the moves whilst secretively whispering to each other.

'So, Scarlett, how's it going with Mr Right, that guy you liked?'

'Oh, not so well, I'm afraid to say.'

'Why? What happened?'

'Well, it all went a bit Mr Wrong really. I ate him yesterday.'

'What?' The voice became louder with shock.

'Shhhhh! Keep it down. I don't want everyone to hear.'

The chin-wagging returned to whispering level, 'Why? Why did you eat him?'

'Well, it was an accident. Really, an accident. One moment we were getting on great and the next I was fondly chomping on his head.'

'But I thought you liked him?'

'I did. Obviously too much,' she giggled. 'That's what us praying mantises do, isn't it? We meet a male, mate with him and then eat him. The mating bit was fun and I tried to resist but the natural gnashing urge was just too strong.'

'Oh well, never mind.'

'Yeah, that's that, I suppose. I really must try

and tame my insatiable appetite.'

'How did he taste?'

'If I'm honest, he tasted de-li-cious. The best male meal I've ever had.'

The pair sniggered and continued their sparring with increased zeal.

Watching all this exercise made Dylan feel sleepy and, as he was alone for the first time on his journey, he opted to climb a nearby tree where he would be camouflaged and safe from predators and hopefully get some much-missed sleep.

He started to ascend in the knowledge that he'd find some tasty leaves to munch when he reached a branch. Half way up the tree trunk a gaggle of geckos frolicked past him, also heading up the tree, all except for one gecko who looked at Dylan and bellowed, 'Oi! Do you mind taking your clumsy claw off my tail?'

'Pardon me,' replied Dylan with embarrassment and lifted his claw to free the gecko that was now separated from the rest of the crowd.

'Wait for me guys!' it said and scampered away at great speed.

By the time Dylan reached the nearest branch the sun was setting and darkness closed in. There was lush vegetation to eat on arrival. There were also, incidentally, insects that looked like vegetation. He picked up what he thought was a leaf and was interrupted by a voice saying, 'What the devil do you think you are doing? Don't you dare even think about it if you know what's good for you. You have no right to eat me. I'm still very much ALIVE!'

Dylan quickly put it back where he found it, flustered and humiliated, and looked more carefully from then on.

He attempted to eat some leaves but they were flavourless to him, as if he was eating old, dry, mouldy tree bark. They gave him no satisfaction at all. Then he surrendered and hung from the branch and tried to nap, but was disturbed by an excruciating noise, soon realising that he had chosen a tree which was hosting a late night gecko party.

There was unbearable chatter and screeching and trunk-thumping as the geckos stomped and jumped and danced and sang. Even being hard of hearing, he could not block out the kerfuffle. They grabbed passing fireflies and swished them in the air like flags, producing a mass of bright flickering lights.

He reminisced about the peace and quiet of his home tree and began to feel deeply lonely. The full moon was large in the sky and glared suspiciously down from above.

A camouflaged chameleon, sharing the branch, had its back to him but swivelled an eye one hundred and eighty degrees to look at him.

It shouted above the din, 'These monthly gecko gatherings can get rather boisterous at times.'

Dylan lifted his eyebrows in agreement but couldn't see the creature who was talking to him. He searched around the immediate area and finally focussed on the brown eye-ball, mounted on wrinkly folds of green skin, staring back at him from the tree bark.

'But I'm not one to talk,' it continued, 'I used to attend such things when I was a boy and was quite the charmer, I can tell you, still got the groovy moves.'

With that it lifted up on its hind legs and wriggled its body about to the throbbing beat, pinching his digits together like they were puppets.

'And check this out for a party piece!'

Its body changed colour from a woody creviced olive green and nutmeg brown to swatches of luminous colour – deep yellows, plush reds and vibrant blues – that pulsed with the ebb and sway of the music.

Dylan was impressed but was not in the mood for entertainment and secretly wished the creature would just go away. His wish was granted as the chameleon, realising that his audience was not enticed, decided to creep off to the party and re-live the good old days, not even bothering to bid the unsociable sloth goodbye.

Alone once again, the annoying sound from the party above fell away as Dylan caught sight of three sloths in the adjacent tree. There were two adults tending to their child and feeding it cecropia leaves. It was a vision that stirred emotions in Dylan that had not bubbled up in him before.

He had always put on a brave face when his parents departed and just got on with things. They just disappeared. The immense rain that usually made him feel alive and fresh now drowned his buoyant spirit. He wept uncontrollably. The rain camouflaged his tears and fell down to the ground, oblivious, filtering his emotion into the soil down below. With every drip he felt lousier and lousier and more and more worthless.

Why did they go? What had he done wrong to cause them to leave? What were they doing now? Would they ever come back? What was his purpose? Would he always be alone? Questions, questions, questions swirled in his head but no answers came and his heart sank silently. He missed the feeling of being held close to his mother's warm heart, protected by her grasp, and he missed his father's playful nature that made him laugh whenever he was awake. Other, older sloths had told Dylan that he looked just like his dad.

The forest didn't feel friendly to Dylan. He was as anonymous as the chameleon. At that moment, a blood-red scorpion thrashed past him on a mission to take away the life of something unsuspecting nearby. Not as though it was a danger to him but it made the forest feel a scary place to be alone.

Dylan had never purposely killed anything, but, in his bleak frame of mind, he was tempted. He lifted a sharp claw, ready to strike the scorpion through the head, but couldn't go through with it. He placed his claw gently back down on the tree bark and allowed the scorpion to scuttle away, unaware how close it had come to death. Killing for no reason wouldn't have made him feel any better.

To add to his misery, he caught a whiff of what smelled like rotting flesh. Of all the branches in all the trees, he swivelled his head to look below and realised that he had parked himself just above a carrion flower. It looked like a raw set of lungs with a yellow flower in the middle. The vile stench was only appreciated by flies, who were fooled by the smell and flew into the middle to meet with the gruesome death of slow liquidation.

Dylan squeezed his nostrils together and only released them to inhale air when absolutely necessary. He couldn't be bothered to move anywhere and yearned to be back in his familiar world, or perhaps out of the forest altogether, and cried until his body was exhausted and shivering. He desperately desired to meet Viva again. Every time he closed his eyes images of his mother and father flashed onto his inner eyelids and he stirred wide-eyed, always awake.

There was no respite from it.

Eventually, images of his parents were replaced with images of Viva, and his eyelids seemed more peaceful. Still, though, his muscles ached and he couldn't sleep. He just rested his mind and hung from the branch listening to the rain.

CHAPTER SIX
The Dark Debacle

Dylan roused from his rest to an unusual sight. His head seemed to be in a dark cave with a big juicy berry at the end of it. Now, sloths don't do anything quickly but, in this instance, Dylan did. He realised that the juicy berry was not what he first thought it to be, but was in fact a dangling tonsil within the large mouth of a hungry and extremely big cat.

He snapped his head back, just in time, before the attacker closed his jaws and he found himself face to face with his most feared predator. He was trembling but knew he had to talk and talk fast if he wasn't to be eaten.

'What do you think you're doing?' demanded Dylan to the sinister character.

'I'm having you for dinner,' replied the black cat with intense auburn eyes.

He continued, licking his lips, 'We don't get many sloths around here, so you are a bit of a delicacy for me.'

Dylan could feel his blood rush to his face and his heart beat in his throat. He had a surge of courage and used his long claws to swipe the cat around the face, causing it to let out an enormous roar of pain: 'Ouch! Owwww!'

The claw marks bled down its cheek.

'Now, that really wasn't necessary.' The beast, quickly composed again, spoke in a distinguished, husky tone.

'Look what you've done to my flawless face. I can't show myself to any other big cat until it's healed or they'll laugh at me for being beaten up by a slow, harmless, and rather pathetic sloth. We jaguars have a reputation of being top predator to uphold.'

Dylan breathed a sigh of relief now that he was not going to be made into cat food.

'Are you sure you are a jaguar?' Dylan quizzed.

'What do you mean by that?'

'Well, I was taught that jaguars had spots, a bit like leopards. You know, with a gold and brown spotted appearance. But there aren't any spots on you.'

'Well observed,' the cat replied patronisingly, 'and your point is, exactly?'

'Oh nothing, nothing at all.'

'Okay, er, yeah scientifically jaguars are mostly of the spotted variety but I have a rare fur condition which means I'm all black. You can see the spots if you look close enough.'

'Aren't panthers all black?'

'Yes, correct, but I can assure you that I'm one

hundred and one percent jaguar. I should know. I've behaved like one all of my life.'

'Okay, I accept your explanation. Thanks for clearing that up.'

'Here, feel my fur. It's the most luxurious in the forest,' the cat boasted, encouraging Dylan to stroke him.

Dylan couldn't resist the temptation to touch it and concluded, 'So it is.'

He felt proud for sticking up to the big bully and grinned with relief now that he'd learnt that the jaguar wasn't as tough as he first thought.

'What are you sniggering at?' asked the deflated feline, whilst licking his paw and carefully stroking it over the ear and sleekly down his cheek three times.

'Oh, nothing,' replied Dylan smugly. 'I was thinking, well, if you're not going to front your buddies for a while, how about adopting me as a part-time friend and heading towards Lake Aromatza? I'm trying to find a butterfly acquaintance of mine, who is conducting an important forest investigation. She is absolutely marvellous and...'

'Okay, you big ball of hair, there's no need to bore me with the details at this point. Save the spiel,' he intervened abrasively but then changed tack. 'A sloth and a jaguar, huh? How odd.'

He stroked his face and preened his whiskers before announcing his decision. 'I suppose a short trek through the jungle will help me heal my wounds and recuperate from that unpleasant surprise. You're on!'

They grinned at each other and then Dylan introduced himself, 'I'm Dylan.'

'I'm Jules,' replied the jaguar.

'Great, that's that then. But promise me that I'm no longer on your menu,' Dylan said with a hint of sarcasm.

'Oh, I'm not brave enough to risk another swipe. However, before we depart for Lake Aromatza, I must get a take away meal somewhere else. I feel peckish.'

Dylan nodded in agreement but stated, 'Do your hunting far away from here because I don't want to watch you.'

Jules raised himself onto all four paws, stretched backward and forward, and sleekly manoeuvred down the tree, 'I'll return soon having satisfied my hunger'.

Dylan tried to keep his mind off what Jules was up to and thought of the journey ahead instead, with a new sense of courage. He gave out a big O-shaped yawn and started to descend - at his usual very slow pace - down the tree trunk with his head held high in the air. He reached the bottom in good time and saw Jules approach, licking his lips.

'Scrumptious.'

'Spare me the gory details,' said Dylan, 'I really don't want to know, even if it is what you big cats do. I can smell your breath from here and it reeks of raw flesh. Being of strictly vegetarian constitution suits me just fine and dandy.'

'Yeah, bad breath isn't a perk of being a top predator,' admitted Jules.

He used his mouth to grip Dylan gently by the scruff of his neck, and raised him onto his velvet-textured back.

'Careful, careful!' said a slightly wary Dylan.

It was dusk once again. The cat's movements were sleek and silent through the forest. Every now and then, they would stop for Dylan to collect some leaves on the journey. Dylan learned to hold on tight as the rainforest terrain was unpredictable and the jaguar swiftly leapt over and walked under branches and creepers that crossed their path. The rain was penetrating the forest heavily, as well, but this didn't stop the pair having fun together.

'Wahey!' Dylan yelled, as Jules took an unexpected leap.

'Are you still holding on?' Jules enquired every so often. Occasionally, they would stop suddenly at the sound of a bird giving a sky-piercing squawk or to allow a threatening snake to slither across their path.

'You sure are heavy for a creature that only eats leaves,' commented Jules.

'Yeah, well, we sloths don't do the same amount of exercise as you big cats. You have the whole rainforest to roam in the dark of night and you are well camouflaged for your outings. I, on the other paw, have green algae on me that really restricts me to my tree and I was always nervous to go much further. My body is exhausted, I haven't slept in days. I wonder if you forget how to sleep.'

'I doubt that. Look at you now, dear chap. Look at you now!'

They chuckled together and an electric mood sizzled between them.

'Have you ever heard of the game I-Spy?' Dylan asked.

'Sure have, hasn't everyone?'

'Okay, I'll go first. I-Spy with my bulbous eye something beginning with 'T"

'Trreees?'

'Nope.'

'Tyrannosaurus Rex?'

'Noooooo! They haven't lived in the forest for yonks... centuries.'

'Tarantula?'

'Yes. Well done.'

They slowed down to watch a puffy, hairy, flat-footed spider stroll up a tree trunk nearby and then tiptoe thread by thread into the centre of its delicate web. Then they picked up their pace and travelled on.

'Now your turn to start, Jules.'

'I-Spy with my beady eye something beginning with Oooooh...'

'Orange?'

'No, oooooh, CRIKEY!'

'That doesn't start with an 'O'...'

CHAPTER SEVEN
What's That? That? And THAT?

They looked out at an alien, unwelcoming landscape. All the trees were missing. There was nothing surrounding them but charred vegetation. It was a creepy sight.

Dylan choked, 'Where are we Jules?'

'Sshhhh, Dylan. Be quiet! We must make it through here without being noticed,' instructed Jules. 'I'll move as quietly and quickly as I can and we'll be back in familiar surroundings as soon as possible.'

Jules took every step carefully: toe, sole, heel, toe, sole, heel. The ground was flat and burnt to cinders, and only nothingness remained. Dylan could see out of the corner of his eye small areas of whipping flames. The sound of crackling fire echoed across the entire area. There was no sign of any life at all, apart from the bats swooping overhead plucking insects from the air. It was a feast for them, and an abundance of bats joined the feeding frenzy. Hundreds, maybe thousands.

Dylan laid his head on Jules' back and wished that they were not so conspicuous against the barren background, shorn of any camouflaging plant life. He could sense the bats flying closely around him and feared that one might lose its navigational skills and collide with them. A chill shuddered through his body.

Jules, meanwhile, was concentrating on guiding them stealthily out of this bleak environment unnoticed. A cold wind swirled around the open plain. The air was thin and hazy, causing them to wheeze as they crept along. Dylan had a ghastly bitter taste in his mouth from inhaling fumes.

All was going well until some ashes swished up Dylan's nose and…

'Aaaatcheew!'

Jules stopped in his tracks and remained still for what seemed an age, although in reality it was probably only moments.

'Who goes there?' squeaked a high-pitched voice.

Before they had a chance to reply, a chorus of voices screeched altogether:

'Who goes there?' 'Who goes there?' 'Who goes there?' 'Who goes there?' 'Who goes there?' 'Who goes there?' 'Who goes there?' 'Who goes there?' 'Who goes there?' 'Who goes there?' 'Who goes there?' 'Who goes there?'

The volume was piercing.

Jules took in a deep breath and roared, 'Silence!

I shall explain if you'll let me.'

The area fell silent, apart from one bat that continued screeching, 'Who goes there?'

'Okay, Hattie, you can stop now,' instructed another bat. 'We've made our point.'

Jules looked up at the bats overhead. Their delicate wings flapped and suspended their bodies in mid air. Although they flew elegantly, their faces were by no means beautiful. In fact, they grimaced menacingly at all times. Their ears were disproportionately large compared with the rest of their petite, squashed facial features, and they stuck perkily upwards like sails.

'I am Jules, the jaguar, and this is my friend Dylan, the sloth. I assure you that we mean no harm but have lost our way. We need to get to Lake Aromatza and seem to have taken a wrong turn. If you would be as kind as to point us the way out of here, we'd be much obliged.'

One of the bats responded, 'Quickest way is to take a left past the next set of flames and go straight from there. This is not a place for you to be. Take my advice and hurry!'

'Thank you. We will be on our way.'

'But before we go,' Dylan piped up, 'What has happened here? Why is there so much gloom and emptiness?'

Once again a tidal wave of sound erupted from the bats.

'The humans!' 'The humans!' 'The humans!' 'The

humans!' 'The humans!' 'The humans!' 'The humans!'
'The humans!' 'The humans!' 'The humans!'

'Sssshh,' demanded the dominant bat.

He spoke on behalf of all of them, 'The humans were here a few days ago. They cut down the trees and burnt the remains of the vegetation so that they can set up camp here for cattle grazing or something. The relentless noise denied me a decent sleep for days. With my poor sight, I couldn't see what they were up to after dark, but I did hear the ruckus with my own ears.'

The bat continued, 'To be honest, though, it has benefited us bats very nicely. There are so many insects in these parts nowadays - mmm, a real bat banquet. But hurry, it's time you were leaving.'

The sound of wings flapping multiplied and the bats swooped through the air in organised chaos.

Jules continued to walk carefully towards the flame burning in front of them. He stubbed his toe on a hard object which made him lose his balance and stumble forwards but he managed to stay upright.

They both looked behind to see what the obstruction was and caught sight of a white long bone amongst the ashes. Without a word, too petrified to talk, they scanned the area. The lone bone was actually surrounded by many of various sizes, scattered in the darkness. Snakes slithered and knotted themselves through the eye sockets of skulls as if they were playground objects. It was impossible to tell what creatures the bones had once belonged to but it was evidence of the beings that once teemed in this now barren, soulless land.

All of a sudden, the bats departed from the night sky above, and an enormous shadow descended over-head. It was an eagle with broad wings and it regally dived towards Dylan. Its golden eyes flickered with determination and its long talons grasped him by the shoulders and began to lift him from Jules' back.

'Aaaarrrggghhhh! Jules! Help! He's got me in his grip.'

Jules turned around and saw Dylan in the ea-gle's mighty grasp. He had no time to think and leapt up and grabbed Dylan by the waist, starting a tug of war. The eagle let out a fierce squawk but Jules held on tight.

'Don't worry Dylan. I've got you!'

The battle commenced… back… forth… back… forth with extraordinary strength.

But the eagle did not surrender and continued to rip at Dylan's shoulders. Tears streamed down Dylan's face, terrified of where the eagle was going to take him and what he would do with him. He could hear his own heart pumping between his ears and his internal organs rattled around inside him.

Jules looked the eagle directly in the eyes and roared, 'He's with me. Now, let go, you feathered freeaaaaak!'

The eagle was shocked and loosened its grip momentarily, then unveiled its wings. It decided that this prey was protected and flew off in search of an easier abduction.

Dylan was free. He hugged Jules. His tears flowed freely and unashamedly.

'There, there, little one,' Jules said. 'You're alright now. Nothing is going to hurt you. The eagle has gone and I won't let anything hurt you again. Okay?'

Dylan's crying ceased and he wiped his face. 'T-t-t-terrifying! Thanks, Jules. You saved my life. Words cannot express my feelings.'

Jules replied, 'Oh, I'm not very good with this sentimental stuff, but winning battles is a privilege that top predators have. That debacle gave me a bit of an adrenalin rush, actually. Climb back on and let's get going again. We still have a way to go and no time to waste.'

Dylan climbed back on and told Jules, 'You really are a special friend.'

Jules smiled as to return the compliment but his pride took over and he said, 'Enough of that. Away we go!'

Once again they were running through the forest, now avoiding bones and amber embers on the ground instead of the green creeper vines that once hugged around the trees. The flames looked spectacular against the dark night sky. The vivid orange, red and yellow colours entwined and twirled amongst the bleak surroundings. Dylan wondered how something so mesmerising and full of life could cause so much destruction.

They followed the bats' directions, and veered

left past the smouldering pyres to continue on their journey.

After some time, the pair moved back into the familiar sights and smells of the forest. White orchids welcomed them on either side of the path. Their long slender petals, like elegant fingers, beckoned at them. The fragrances, dominated by eucalyptus and bursting with exotic sweet flowers, seemed intense to Dylan's neglected nostrils and made him dizzy.

The celebration of colour seduced their eyes. Dylan made an effort to look more intently at each tree that he saw. In one glance there must have been over ten different types of flowers and splashes of coloured petals everywhere, waving at him as if to welcome him back to familiarity. The contrasting colours and sizes of the green, brown, auburn, yellow, orange, white, golden leaves, the height and girth and texture of the tree trunks and the scurrying wildlife that lived amongst them were all freshly intriguing to him now.

Jules walked over to some cream-coloured flowers with light yellowish-orange fruits, parked himself down and said, 'Pick yourself some mullaca leaves over there, they will help your damaged shoulders to heal.'

Dylan dangled down and swiped a handful of leaves and fruits. He ate some of the sweet fruits, for medicine, and positioned some leaves on his weeping shoulders. They would keep the wounds clean and prevent infection setting in.

'Hey, Jules, I've got a magic trick to show you.'

Jules turned his head to look at Dylan who was clutching a leaf in his hand.

'You see this white powdered fungi growing on this leaf?'

'Yeah,' replied Jules, curious.

'Well, if you rub it together… Look!' Dylan rubbed the fungi between two of his claws and the powder turned to a red liquid.

'Voila! Magic!' he said and painted a red streak on either side of Jules' face, from his nose across each jowl. He did the same to himself and together the pair looked like warriors of the forest. They grinned.

Then they were on the move again.

CHAPTER EIGHT
A Sight for Bulbous Eyes

The hours ticked by. Jules was starting to tire. His head was not so proudly poised as before and his whole body drooped downwards under gravity, lacking prowess. The early birds started to warble melodies accompanied by the busy routine of insects scurrying along invisible highways. Just when Jules was going to surrender to his aching body, THERE IT WAS, straight in front of them: a vast area of glassy blue lake. The breeze teased the water, creating soft waves.

It was Lake Aromatza.

'Do you see what I see?' yelped Dylan, who was unable to contain his excitement.

'Certainly do.'

The sun was rising over the lake and parrots were swooping above, forming silhouettes against the opaque sky. Peace and tranquillity filled the air. Dylan was speechless. He also felt anxious, as he still had to somehow find Viva.

'Stop right where you are!' ordered a voice from above.

Perched on a branch was a very prim multi-coloured military macaw. Dylan admired his impressive plumage of green, yellow, light blue, red and black.

The moment didn't last long, as they were encircled by hundreds of tiny yet menacing poison arrow frogs. Their colours, vibrant shades of red, blue, green or yellow, all seemed to scream 'Danger!'

The military macaw squawked, 'You are surrounded by an army equipped with enough poison mucus on their skins to kill you almost instantly, so no sudden moves.'

Dylan pleaded, 'But I am looking for a dear friend who said she was heading this way.'

'No can do, I'm afraid. This is the end of your journey, ambitious one. That over there is a human village and I would not be doing my job properly if I were to let you put yourselves in grave danger by going any further,' he explained. 'Many have gone and never returned.'

Dylan looked at the human village in the distance on the adjacent side of the lake, with the distant outlines of mountains behind.

He saw no trees, but rather wooden structures. He saw human creatures standing on two limbs, rather than four, taller and more stretched than himself. Smaller humans ran around with smiles on their faces making strange, squeaky noises. The taller ones were walking to and from the lake with large buckets of water on their heads. They looked harmless enough. They didn't have long claws like him or sharp teeth like his friend Jules. Nor did they have bodies covered in slimy mucus. However, he had to trust the macaw's judgement and face the realisation that his journey could go no further.

Jules addressed Dylan, 'Well, I suppose that's that then, dear chap. Sorry! Nowhere else for us to travel or we'd be in serious danger. No adventure or butterfly is worth that.'

Dylan sulked, 'She was kind of special though. But you're right, I need to think sensibly.'

A giant metallic blue butterfly fluttered by him but he hardly noticed it. Grey clouds, like saturated sponges, filled the sky above Lake Aromatza. They hung heavily and then with a sigh of relief opened to free their excess water. Rain started to pour down over the lake, followed by an enormous clap of thunder and lightning that sliced through the murky sky and arrowed to the ground. Everything felt heavy and ominous. His heart sunk into his empty stomach, his body was sapped of energy and his mind was deprived of hope.

The poison arrow frogs dispersed under the shelter of leaves. Dylan's thick hair was designed to be waterproof and he decided to clamber off Jules and slump on the ground to watch the hive of activity in the human village. It was compulsive viewing even through his sore, tired eyes.

Jules told Dylan, 'I'm just going off to find a quick meal and when I return we should perhaps make tracks home, dear chap.'

Dylan sat and watched, curious. The unfamiliar creatures were running into their wooden structures, obviously not as well adapted as him to the rain. His head dropped in disappointment, as there was not a wonderful butterfly in sight anywhere.

'All this effort for nothing,' he mumbled, dispirited.

CHAPTER NINE
Revived

Dylan had never felt so lost.

He longed, again, to be back in the comfort of his homeland surrounded by friendly faces, amongst the familiar flora and fauna of the forest.

Then, through all the gloom, came a twinkling sensation. He looked up and there she was, balancing delicately once again on his snout.

She flew to his ear and said, 'Hello stranger. What are you doing in this part of the forest? Surely, this is no place for a sleepy sloth?'

Dylan's eyes sparkled like marbles and he rose to his feet, flailing his arms about in joy, 'Wow, I've found you. I've really found you. I came all this way to find you and that's really you. Here you are.'

Viva interrupted Dylan's rambling, 'Yep, it sure is me… same old me. Now answer my question!'

She smiled inquisitively.

'To be honest, Viva, as soon as you left me I couldn't sleep very well. Actually, I couldn't sleep at all. I was curious about what was happening to the forest after losing my home. You had such a unique attitude and I realised that I couldn't just sit and wait for you to return with news, so I thought I'd catch up with you instead.'

'Bravo, Dylan! That was awfully brave and a bit risky for one who doesn't know his way around these parts.'

'Well, I took the chance because I just felt so unsettled. I have met some incredibly helpful and insightful creatures along the way.'

'Sounds like you've done just fine on your own then,' Viva said, clapping her wings in a celebratory flutter.

Dylan recalled, 'There were a few risky episodes, I must admit. For instance my friend Jules, a jaguar, and I lost our way and strayed into a burnt barren part of the forest by mistake. It was extremely eerie. There was hardly any life there at all. Ghastly and ghostly. Only bats snacking on the mass of insects available. Oh, and I nearly got abducted by an angry eagle but Jules scared it away and saved my life.'

Viva shook her head, concerned, 'Yikes! You must stay well away from those parts. Promise me that you'll never go there again. It's dangerous no matter how forest-wise you are.'

Dylan said with conviction, 'I certainly won't go anywhere near there again, Viva. You have my word. But on the plus side, I've had so much fun and enlightenment on my jaunt. I only wish I could be as mobile and elegant as you.'

'Ah, but you have your own gifts and talents, Dylan, that's what makes this forest so fascinating and diverse. It would be rather boring if we were all the same.'

Dylan continued, 'And Lake Aromatza is the most enchanting sight that I've ever seen. Flabber-gasting! Oh, which reminds me, while we are on the subject of talents, I have discovered a talent of my own. Two, actually. Firstly, a kind caiman taught me how to swim so I could get across the river.'

'Splendid, replied Viva, 'a swimming sloth too! I'll have to watch you in action some time. Butterflies can't swim so you have one up on me there. Now, what's your other recently discovered talent?'

'Err, you may not like this one so much,' he gulped.

'Why? What is it?'

'You must promise that you won't think of me badly and you'll still like me after I tell you.'

'Okay.'

'No, you must say that you promise.'

'Okay, I promise. Now tell me what is it.'

'Well, it turns out that my hair contains oodles of parasites and other bugs that are irresistible to oth-er hungry beings.'

'Goodness gracious! That's gross, Dylan. Do they live on your body all the time?'

'Yep, and I didn't even know until now. Some

primate mates that I met along the way couldn't get enough of the sloth cuisine. You promised that you'd still like me the way that I am. I mean this is the way I was made, right?'

'Don't worry, Dylan. I still think you're as handsome as ever, even with creepy crawlies that make me heave. On some level it is quite charitable to give them such a welcoming home.'

'Thank you, Viva. That means a lot to me. Would you mind if I asked you something more personal?'

'Sure, go ahead,' she replied.

'What was your childhood like, Viva?'

'Why do you ask, Dylan?'

'Well, when I had some time on my own I saw a happy family of sloths and it got me thinking about my own childhood and how I was abandoned by my parents while I was asleep one day. I have fond memories of my mother's nurturing and love for me. She used to hold me tightly, feed me the best leaves from the tree and my father used to tickle me with feathers under my nose and on the padded soles of my paws. The memories took me to a bleak place and it has left me blaming myself for their actions. Could I have done anything different, do you think?'

Viva looked down and then back at him, 'Oh Dylan, that is a sad tale, but you must not blame yourself in any way for their actions. It was out of your control.'

She continued softly, 'You will never find the answers that you seek, but you were fortunate enough to know them at all. As a caterpillar I was one of an enormous family and didn't know my mother and father. You were expected to go your own way from day one. You were expected to form a chrysalis, and have a mystical metamorphosis and turn into what I am today. It was all quite enigmatic really.

'I do remember seeing a message written in silver on the inside wall of my chrysalis, which advised me about life in one sentence. It read, "Don't let anyone or anything take your twinkle away from you." I felt very special and inspired by that until I spoke to other butterflies about it and learned that every chrysalis has that written inside it, or something very similar of the sort, which was pretty annoying.

'Oh, well, what can you do? Not knowing my parents was just the way it was: the natural wonder of my species. Wallowing in the what-if state of mind will get you nowhere in life. Nope, I'm just grateful that I am alive and able to embrace it. Dwelling on the past is not a habit that I wish to accommodate. That is not to say that it is wrong for you to deal with your pain. Perhaps one day when you have a family it will make more sense to you. Does that answer your question, Dylan?'

'Yes Viva. You have a gift of putting things into perspective.'

'And don't ever forget that you are surrounded by creatures that do care about you and that you care about them. Nothing in this world is more valuable than that. We are part of this forest and should make the most of it. If it will cheer you I will flutter my wings under your nose and on the pads of your paws.'

Viva smiled mischievously. She flew to his snout and fluttered her wings speedily, tenderly brushing it, causing Dylan to laugh so much that his stomach muscles were in joyful agony.

'Okay, okay. Enough! Enough already! You are so right, of course, I will stop my selfish ruminating and get back to the bigger picture and the serious business of finding out what is going on in these here parts. I'd never seen humans before. Are they a rare species?'

Viva whispered, 'As you know, that's why I'm here. I have to do some detective work, you see. They are rare to the forest but rumour has it that more and more are moving in and taking up spaces usually home to other creatures. Pretty alarming, really.'

'They don't look very scary to me,' said Dylan, 'with no claws, sharp teeth or mucus. Can I come with you on your secret mission?'

'Oh, don't underestimate them. They have these huge machines that aren't scared of anything. They are the biggest, most bombastic things you've ever seen and have no fear at all. I could do with your help but you really are too clumsy and indiscreet for my type of work. How about staying here? I'll get back to you when I've done some more investigating.'

Dylan was a little nervous that she wouldn't return, 'Promise, you'll come back?'

'I promise, Dylan. Now, you really must try and

get some proper shut-eye.'

'Oh, I've tried really hard,' Dylan groaned, 'but have failed so far. I think it'll come back to me naturally when I'm back in a tree that I consider home. Until then I'll just have to droop and bear it.'

She smiled and flew off towards the human village.

Jules returned a few minutes later. Dylan glowed with happiness and Jules could sense that something had happened during his absence.

'What's been going on, dear chap, for you to be looking so pleased with yourself?'

Dylan gave a wide smile and told Jules about his reunion with Viva, concluding, 'You see, she managed to find me just when all my hope of meeting her again had vanished.'

'This forest is full of surprises,' responded Jules.

'We must wait for a while until she returns. She's got a bit of undercover work to do regarding that human village, okay?'

'Okey dokey. That's fine with me, young one. I could do with a snooze.'

Jules retired to the base of a nearby tree and Dylan rested on the big cat's velvety, luxurious, pillow-like middle and closed his eyes. His muscles relaxed and melted downwards, in the knowledge that he was protected.

Jules slept deeply and snored loudly. The noise agitated the military macaw above on the branch and he tutted with frustration as he kept watch at his station, and rolled his eyes at the uncouth cat and unkempt sloth below.

CHAPTER TEN
Friend, No, Foe

Both were blissfully wrapped up in a blanket of warmth by the daily sunshine. Jules slept all day but, once again, Dylan just lay with his eyes closed, awake, and smiling.

For a second he thought he was in his home territory but when he opened his eyes and as things came into view he remembered where he was. His head, resting on Jules' stomach, was slowly moving up and down in time with the big cat's deep breaths.

He rubbed his eyes and yawned, sat up and appreciated the magnificent evening sunset of vivid layers: reds, oranges, yellows and slices of purples and blues. He selected some leaves from the ground for a well-deserved snack. He even tried to eat a few berries to see if he might grow to like them and make his diet a bit more interesting. He actually started to enjoy their sweet juice.

From a distance Dylan spotted Viva flying his way. He watched her zigzag elegantly towards him and within a few minutes she landed on his snout.

She didn't seem to be twinkling as brightly as normal and Dylan enquired, 'Are you okay, Viva? You look upset.'

'I'm in shock,' she replied, 'I've just overheard the most awful, AWFUL, just dreadful news.'

She took a deep breath and continued, 'It seems that the humans are going to chop down the trees where you live and export them abroad to make furniture, then turn the land into a farming plot...'

'What's furniture?' Dylan butted in.

'Well, like you have a tree to sleep in, a branch to sit on and so on and so forth, and the humans need trees for that purpose too. Apparently there are more and more humans needing trees for this and that. Then they are going to turn the area into farms and houses for more humans to live.'

'That can't be true,' said Dylan, 'What can we do?'

Viva said sadly, 'There's not much we can do. The humans are too tough for us to fight. This is a matter of urgency as they are starting in two days. We must return and make sure all the neighbouring wildlife in the area is safely evacuated because I don't even want to think of the horrific devastation that could occur otherwise.'

Dylan turned to Jules, 'Wake up! Wake up!'

Jules yawned sleepily and smiled, but his smile turned to an angry frown as Dylan explained animatedly what Viva had discovered.

'Sorry, did I hear you right?' asked Jules. 'Did I just hear you correctly? The humans are planning to knock down the area where you live? Surely we should stay and fight!'

Viva flew to Jules' ear and interrupted, 'Hi, I'm Dylan's friend, Viva, but we don't have time for formal introductions so I'll get to the crux. There's no point in trying to battle the humans. They have huge forest-eating machines and I've heard stories like this before in other parts of the rainforest. Sadly, the creatures of the rainforest never win, no matter how hard they try. Now we must get back quickly so to warn the others. Come on!'

Dylan suggested, 'Perhaps staying anywhere in the rainforest won't be enough. Should we think of moving out altogether, to the desert or something?'

'That's crazy!' Jules and Viva responded in stereo.

Viva explained, 'The humans have needs but they are not stupid, from what I can gather. They know that they need to look after the rainforest to survive, as we do. Its breathing trees keep their air clean, its wood and other materials are needed for their everyday lives: food, furniture and warmth to name just a few. I'm convinced that they know how important it is to get the balance right for their survival too. They consider themselves the custodians of the Earth and I'm, um, sure that they know that upsetting the equilibrium would not benefit them in the long run. Well, that's what I'm guessing anyway.

Who knows? But it doesn't change your predicament now, does it? We must think about ourselves. Now, up, up and away we go! And no more radical talk of desert living, you silly thing.'

They rose to their feet and Dylan mounted Jules with difficulty, jumping so that his stomach landed on Jules' slippery back and swung his left hind limb over laboriously. Jules whipped his nose under Dylan's bottom and indignantly put him in riding position. Before he could even get comfortable they were on the move and Jules was sprinting mighty speedily as Viva flew slightly ahead.

'She's a feisty friend, you've got there,' Jules said to Dylan.

'Yes, she's very passionate about saving the forest. It's admirable that something so small and dainty could have such a big heart and care so much,' Dylan replied.

Jules leapt over any branches and creepers that crossed their path and swerved around anything that was in the way, declaring, 'EMERGENCY! Coming through!'

Dylan held on tightly as his body was thrown from left to right. Everything in sight became streaks of colours. Jules panted heavily but continued through the forest with determination, until...

'Ouch!' he yelped and ground to a sudden halt. He had ripped this foreleg against a tree that had giant protruding spikes covering its gothic bark.

Dylan slipped off his back to enable Jules to inspect the gash. He ate some nearby leaves while he waited. Jules licked the bleeding wound, whimpering.

'Are you okay to carry on?' asked Dylan concerned.

'I'll be just fine. Give me a little time to rest and we can get going again.'

They sat together, while Viva sipped nectar from the inviting array of brightly coloured, aromatic flowers. But to Dylan, the repetitive screeching of nearby crickets sounded like an alarm and reinforced the urgency to keep moving. He was anxious.

Dylan told Jules, his eyes wide with longing, 'I've never lived anywhere else but my home tree. It's so unfair that I won't be staying there any longer. Why did this have to happen to me?'

Jules looked over at Dylan with a sympathetic look on his face. 'I know it isn't easy for you, dear chap, but it's just one of those things in life. I've never had a tree to call my own and have always roamed through the forest so I can't really understand what it must be like. However, you have happy memories of your life there. Maybe it's time for a change anyway? I'm sure you'll make the next place home too.'

With that, Jules grabbed Dylan by the neck and swung him onto his back. He was up and running again. Viva looked around, sucked some last-minute nectar and shrieked, 'Wait for me, guys!' and flew up beside them.

The inevitable sunrise went barely noticed and it was daytime again.

Jules' pace had slowed somewhat.

'I'm exhausted,' he moaned. 'I can feel every muscle in my body ache. I may have to stop soon.'

'No way!' intervened Viva. 'You can't stop now; we've almost reached the river.'

As she spoke the river came into view.

'There it is!' exclaimed Dylan pointing ahead.

Viva flew straight across the dividing water, encouraging the others, 'Come on you two!'

Jules looked at Dylan, 'Go ahead, dear chap. You can swim but I shall wait for a Caiman Cab. I'll catch up with you.'

The conversation was interrupted.

'There you are Jules!' said a golden-spotted jaguar, approaching them.

It was chunkier than Jules, with raging eyes positioned close together.

Dylan shuddered.

'Oh, hi, Max,' said Jules, cowering backwards.

'You are on the missing list, Jules. The jaguars' singles scene has been looking for you. So glad I've finally found you. What on Earth are you up to?'

Max was baffled and scanned Dylan from head to paw. Realising there was a problem, Viva flew back across the water to Dylan's side, where she hid under a leaf, ear wigging.

'This is my friend Dylan,' Jules said. 'It's a long story but I've been helping this sloth with some forest issues.'

'Mm-hmm,' responded Max suspiciously. 'You are now mixing with tree-dwellers, hey? What next?'

'Don't be like that, Max,' Jules tried to continue, but…

'The number one rule of being a top predator is not to befriend our prey. Where would the jaguar species be if we ALL did what you are doing, Jules? They belong up in those trees and we belong on the ground and on the lower branches. That is just the way it is.'

'Oh, you really shouldn't have such a low opinion of yourself,' quipped Dylan, trying to lighten the mood.

But Max was not amused and glared right through him with disdain, as though he were invisible.

'Come on, Max, I haven't committed the worst crime by helping out the sloth.'

'Pah, I'm sure it's very admirable but now it's time to return to your own. If you come now I will keep this madness between you and me. Otherwise I will be forced to alert others from the jaguar population and you will be considered an outcast. That is the choice.'

Jules turned to Dylan.

'He's right, I'm afraid. Sorry, I must go back to what I know,' he said with a nervous twitch in his left eye.

'Surely not,' pleaded Dylan, 'there must be a way

that we can be together. I've never been so close to anyone before.'

'If there was, dear chap, I would do it. But this is the end of the road for me. As much as I have enjoyed your company, we are just too different. We have our own identities and our own responsibilities which cannot and must not be compromised.'

Dylan was speechless and touched Jules on his right shoulder, then sadly said, 'I understand. I understand. It's just so unfair. We've been through so much together. I don't know what I'll do without you.'

'You'll be fine. You've changed so much in the time I've known you, and have become much more courageous. Now, go and do what you have to do. I'm sorry we have to part this way.'

'I'm sure we can meet up some time in the future, though, right?'

'No Dylan. This is it. We must look back at what we had as something really unique and special but we have no future friendship. I will avoid your area and will never forget you. Take best care and have a peaceful life.'

'Let's go!' Max ordered impatiently. 'We've got some juicy hunting to do.'

Jules licked Dylan's face with his bristly tongue, then turned and followed Max into the forest. His tail dragged along the ground. He didn't look back.

Dylan shouted, 'You were brilliant Jules!'

The regret echoed through the forest.

Then he was gone.

Dylan felt honoured to have known Jules, but crushed about the unchangeable circumstances at the same time. His heart felt empty and plummeted to the pit of his stomach, like a dull pebble.

He sighed, then looked up to the sky and clambered into the river swallowing a grotesque gulp of water. There was no time to waste and he swam, without even thinking about what his arms and legs should be doing. He brushed against a large green lily pad meditating on the water. All he could think about was the need to reach his area as soon as possible. When he reached the far riverbank, he dragged himself breathlessly out of the water and collapsed on the grass.

Viva flew by Dylan's ear and shouted as loudly as she could, 'You've got to keep going Dylan. I know you're tired but I'm too small for the residents to hear me, so come on, keep going!'

Dylan could hardly breathe, let alone speak, but panted, 'Can you find me some travel assistance to get me there, as you know how slow I am on land?'

'I'll be back in a moment,' she said and flew off.

A while later two chunky dark-haired howler monkeys with long twisty limbs and large hands appeared in front of him. Without a word they lifted Dylan up on one shoulder each and strode like cowboys towards the base of a tree.

Viva appeared and explained to Dylan, 'These

monkeys, Woolly and Plucky, will help you move quickly through the forest and I'll be right behind you.'

Then, a chain of monkeys attached from neck to tail lowered from the trees, grabbed Dylan, and wrenched him to the height of the third branch.

'Here we go!' howled one of the monkeys. 'Geronimo!'

Dylan shouted, 'Pppppardon?' but he was ignored.

One of the monkeys took hold of Dylan's upper left limb and the other grabbed the right. They swung him over the gap between the trees to two other monkeys who grabbed him on the other side. There were six monkeys in total and as they swung Dylan, they moved ahead to another tree in a perfectly choreographed routine. They built up momentum and became more confident.

Dylan felt petrified.

'Aaaarrrrggghhhh!' he bellowed every time he thought he was going to fall painfully to the forest floor. But he never did, as the monkeys kept up a strict rhythmical motion. Occasionally they became a bit overconfident for his liking and Dylan was tossed into the air, performed an unexpected summersault and was then caught on his descent. It was only fortunate that he didn't have a belly full of food or he would have felt queasy by now.

Viva flew ahead to investigate the area that was going to be chopped down.

Meanwhile, the monkeys seemed to be having a lot of fun whooping in the trees and using the floppy sloth as a play object, making noises like, 'Wahey!' 'Woo-hoo!' 'Here he comes.' 'Over to you.'

It was broad daylight and all the creatures of the forest watched in astonishment at the entertainment whizzing through the treetops.

CHAPTER ELEVEN
Breaking News

It must have been early afternoon when the monkeys stopped tossing Dylan from branch to branch, and rested him in a familiar place. Dylan couldn't think straight due to all the spinning he had been through. Gradually his faculties recovered and he felt a warm sensation deep down inside himself as he realised that he was in a tree in his home territory.

He let out a deep sigh, 'A-ha, home sweet home.'

His tiredness was all-consuming because he had been awake for countless hours, unthinkable for a sloth. There was no time for idleness as he remembered that by tomorrow this wouldn't be his home any longer. He had lived a simple life in his home area and felt nervous to leave. Would another tree be the same? Would he still have friends nearby? Would there be enough food to go round? But before he had time to wallow, along came Viva.

'Right!' she said assertively. 'I've flown around and scoped out the area where the trees will soon be knocked down. The trees have got a white line paint-ed on them and I have to tell you that, regretfully, there are quite a lot to be felled. Now, as you know, I only have a tiny voice so it's up to you to inform all the creatures within shouting distance. I'll fly and tell the rest that won't hear, on the perimeter.'

'You've got to be joking,' panicked Dylan, who felt like fainting. 'I've never done any public speaking in my life.'

'You'll be fine,' she said, comforting him. 'Speak clearly, keep to the point, no waffling, and tell all those who are speed-challenged not to worry because we have a travel support team on hand. The monkeys are gathering recruits so tell them to wave a large bright flower when they are ready to make a move. Don't worry; no-one will be left behind. The fireflies will light up the path to follow through the forest to the new area.'

With that, she flew off, stopped for a second and gave a wink in Dylan's direction, then fluttered away.

Dylan was left alone and felt very anxious. He took a long look around him and remembered all the new experiences and characters he had encountered during his adventure. But this had to be the toughest part: having to break such devastating news to those he lived close to and cared about. He realised that he wouldn't be heard if he was just to shout, with all the daytime activity in the forest. So he resourcefully broke off the end of a hollow branch to use as a megaphone.

He stood up tall, coughed to clear his throat, took a deep breath and spoke.

'Excuse me everyone.'

At first he was totally ignored so he tried again.

'Er, excuse me everyone.'

No response.

He resorted to, 'HEY! OI! QUIET EVERYONE! LISTEN! I HAVE SOMETHING VERY URGENT TO SAY! SILENCE!'

The forest at once fell silent and every pair of eyes surrounding him, of different colours and sizes, looked his way. He felt himself blush but overcame it quickly and continued, 'I regret that I am the bearer of some dreadful news.'

A mumbling noise filled the silent space as creatures started to speculate and seek comfort in their neighbour or friend.

'Come on friends! Please can I have some quiet? We don't have time to waste!' Dylan continued.

'Our area, that we call home, is no longer going to exist as of tomorrow. A dear friend of mine has informed me that the humans are coming to chop down the trees for their own use so we have no choice but to move deeper into the forest and make new homes for ourselves. Please do not panic, but I advise you all to gather anything you need, keep your children close by and start making your way. The fireflies have lit up the path to follow and if you have any queries the butterflies are here to help, so follow their guidance.'

There was a deadly silence and a deep sense of sadness amongst the crowd. The silence was broken by a familiar voice asking Dylan a question. It was his friend, Oscar, with a worried tone in his voice.

'What about slower creatures, like us sloths? We'll never make it in time.'

'Good question, Oscar. Don't worry if you are slow, older or infirm, there will be assistance from the monkeys who will be here soon. Just wave a large brightly coloured flower that can be seen clearly and they will come to your assistance. Now, stay calm but start making your plans please. I hope to catch up with you in our new pastures soon. Take great care all of you!'

There was a round of applause from all who listened to Dylan's speech. He was overwhelmed.

'Thank you for notifying us,' shouted one voice.

'Yeah, cheers neighbour. We would be in real trouble if you hadn't have told us.'

Dylan mildly grinned but responded sternly, 'Now be on your way!'

CHAPTER TWELVE
High and Low

The forest became a hive of activity, with creatures great and small all co-operating together for the exodus. Some prepared food parcels for the journey, while others searched and gathered together their families, calling out for their children.

The sounds of sad goodbyes echoed through the emptying area.

'Best of luck!'

'Hope to see you again in our new home.'

'Stay in touch, Chico y Chica.'

'We'll meet again and we can have a huge celebration.'

Gradually, there was movement. The insects were the first to emigrate. Long lines of ants, termites, woodlice, worms and praying mantises walked, hopped, buzzed or slithered along. The ground-living creatures, such as tapirs, antelopes and snakes lifted their heads and made their way to the new area. The birds of paradise met in flocks and took to the sky, creating a wave of flapping wings. The sloth population and those that could not make the distance independently picked their large brightly coloured flowers and then sat and waited, waving them around in the air, signalling for assistance.

They didn't have to wait too long because from behind Dylan came a vast number of monkeys swinging and howling through the trees. One of them looked his way, gave him a salute and said, 'Leave this to us, mate. We are at your service.'

The monkeys divided into groups and hurried to all the trees that needed their help. Dylan relaxed in the knowledge that all the creatures were on their way.

His neighbour and friend, Oscar, looked at Dylan and said, 'I'll stay here with you until all the area is clear. I think you could do with some company during this difficult time.'

Dylan was grateful to his friend and tears filled his eyes.

'Thank you,' was all he could manage to say.

They sat in silence while the area seemed to grow lonelier and lonelier.

Viva flew to Dylan. He was delighted to see her.

She praised him, 'Well done, young man! Everyone is now safely on their way and some are even starting to arrive in the new area. Now it's time for you and your friend to be making tracks and I'll see you there.'

She looked at him with admiration and flew

back in the direction that she had come from.

Eight monkeys arrived, including the two that Dylan had already met. 'We will be your pilots for the final leg of your journey. Are you ready to get swinging?'

'Give me a minute,' Dylan said sombrely.

He surveyed the area for the last time.

'You know what?' he addressed Oscar, 'This place no longer feels happy and homely without all the creatures of the forest. It's time to bid it farewell.'

Oscar patted Dylan reassuringly on the shoulder.

'Okay, we can go now,' he said, nodding to the monkeys.

The monkeys gathered around the two sloths and grabbed them.

Dylan grinned cheekily at Oscar, 'Hold on tight! You're gonna love it.'

Oscar was the first to be swung from his branch and Dylan shouted from behind, 'Bon voyage!'

Then, it was his turn. He had that familiar sensation of weightlessness through the trees but this time he felt more at ease. The two friends raced through the thick forest, laughing playfully the whole way.

Oscar chuckled, 'So this is how it feels to have the freedom of a bird. Exquisite!'

CHAPTER THIRTEEN
Common Curtsy

T he monkeys slowed and stopped on a low tree branch.

'This is the end of the designated zone. You see, this is the last tree that will be cut down tomorrow,' explained Plucky.

Dylan reached out and touched the tree as if to say 'Goodbye.'

'Let's get swinging!' and they were off again.

They travelled across swathes of forest, and many swings and loops later they came to a standstill.

Woolly instructed Dylan to close his eyes.

'Why?' Dylan asked.

'Just do it!'

So Dylan did as he was told. Woolly rested him down on a branch and Oscar was set down next to him.

'You can open them now.'

Dylan opened his eyes. He saw the most vibrant celebration in the history of the forest.

'Hip, hip, hooooray!'

A mass of creatures had congregated around him, and they cheered with joy. He blushed. There were the familiar faces of those who had lived near him and those he had met on his travels. There were also new faces who were already residents of the area but were only too pleased to welcome the newcomers.

Sandra, the tapir, shouted up to him, 'You are a hero, Dylan. A legend in these here parts.'

This was met with agreement by others, shouting, 'Yes, you are a hero!'

Dylan didn't know how to acknowledge such admiration and shrugged, saying, 'Oh, really it was nothing. Viva is the real heroine in all of this.'

'Hurrah for Viva!' the crowd cheered.

She flew onto Dylan's snout and curtsied to the masses. She basked blatantly in their attention, and mouthed to Dylan, 'How do I look?'

He replied, 'You look glorious. In fact, you look vivacious, Viva.'

She flew up into the air and danced around Dylan's head, and was quickly joined by her happy flying friends who circled around in joyous celebration.

'I think I will flirt with life around here for a while,' she declared.

Dylan looked down to the forest floor and watched the boa constrictors wrapped around the tree trunks, gossiping. He caught sight of the praying mantis group that bowed slowly, and slightly creepily, towards him. The tortoises smiled broadly. The iguanas waved their red chin flaps like victory flags. The acrobatic tamarins and marmosets performed to their largest crowd yet. Even the military macaw flew by and landed on a nearby branch to congratulate Dylan on the evacuation, 'Grand job, young Private. Couldn't have done it better myself.'

The forest was lit up with rejoicing, happy to be safe and together again.

Dylan was overwhelmed by the festivities and his eyes filled up with a few happy tears. Oscar leant over and said, 'Woah, this is unbelievable!'

'Yes, it really is the most spectacular sight, isn't it?'

Goose bumps spread over his body, making his hair stand to attention in a big ball of directionless spikes - not a cool look. Luckily, Plucky the monkey swung down from above and handed him a tree cone and said, 'This is known as a monkey brush. We primates won't go anywhere without one and neither should you.'

Dylan accepted the gift graciously and put it to use straight away, brushing his hair backwards. He then picked a berry from his new tree and handed it to Oscar, 'Hey, try one of these.'

Oscar didn't hesitate to eat it but, like Dylan's first attempt, his unimpressed expression showed that it wasn't quite to his taste.

'Too sweet for me, Chico. Oh, how's about I bunk in the branch just below, if that's okay?'

'It would be a pleasure to share the same residence,' replied Dylan. He grabbed Oscar and hugged him as if he were a sacred tree.

The forest creatures became acquainted with their new surroundings and each other. The bright white crescent moon smiled sideways and the stars glistened and winked in the thick black sky. They reminded Dylan of the brightly intense eyes of Jules and he took a moment to remember his much missed friend. He slowly clawed his way up the bark of the tree leaving all the commotion behind, followed closely by Oscar, until they reached the top. It was a prime vantage point. His bulbous eyes scanned the flourishing canopy and he realised the view was pretty much the same as from his other tree.

The fantastic fiesta below continued through the night. The gleaming copper sun rose easily and shimmered flamboyantly across the horizon. Dylan dangled from his branch. Inhaling a precious breath of air, he closed his eyes and relished the deepest sleep that he had ever had. He was home.